Through Her Own Eyes

Tavra's Journey to Self–Love

Written by Arvat McClaine
Illustrated by Isabella Millet

Letter to Parents, Teachers, and Other Caring Adults

First, I want to applaud you for the work that you do to ensure that our children are exposed to story-telling and works that allow their imaginations to soar! This is the prime time to encourage children to engage their creativity, to be in a state of wonder, and to learn skills and values that will last a lifetime!

Watching our children explore, learn and grow can be quite fascinating. However, we sometimes forget that our children experience real emotions and they may not have the words to properly express themselves.

In this story, Tavra experiences some emotions that she does not know how to deal with. She does get some help along the way and is able to learn an invaluable lesson that will serve her for the rest of her life.

It is my hope that Tavra's journey will help young children who have difficult emotions to realize that they are not alone and that they have the power within to find light and joy.

To help in this regard, I have included two sections at the end of the story: 1.) a Guided Discussion so that you can help your child(ren) to understand and process the story even better; and 2.) a Guided Journal so that your child(ren) can have the opportunity to further express themselves on their own through drawing, writing, and coloring.

Wishing the best for you and your child(ren)!

In Joy,

Arvat McClaine

Dedication:

To Harry, for allowing me the space to learn to love myself and for applauding me as I share this same gift with others.

To Mrs. Amanda McKeithan's First Grade Class at St. Andrews School: A Special Thank You! You helped me with this book more than you know!

All the kids were playing outside, except Tavra. "Nobody loves me! Nobody loves me!" Tavra cried over and over again.

1

One at a time, the other children wandered over to Tavra and said, "I love you, Tavra." But Tavra was too upset to even hear them.

2

Tavra thought about all the reasons no one loved her. One reason was that her three brothers thought that saying mean things to her was funny.

"Get away from us, you buck-toothed beaver!" her brother, Niles, said and they all laughed until their stomachs hurt.

The other girls in the neighborhood were slightly older and so much cooler than Tavra. They knew all the new dances and cheers, like, "We are the mighty, mighty Dragons!"
But Tavra was just a Plain Jane. She didn't know any dances or anything about cheers, so the other girls didn't want Tavra around.

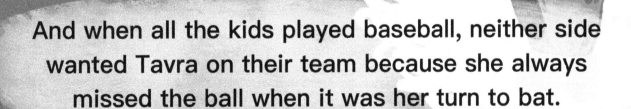

And when all the kids played baseball, neither side wanted Tavra on their team because she always missed the ball when it was her turn to bat.

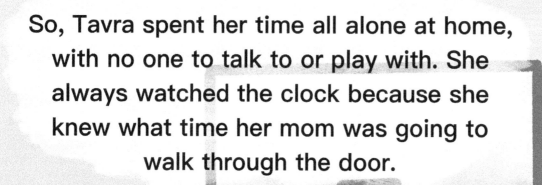

So, Tavra spent her time all alone at home, with no one to talk to or play with. She always watched the clock because she knew what time her mom was going to walk through the door.

"Mama!" she cried out, happy to finally see her mom. "Guess what?" She started to excitedly tell her mom about all of the things that were zooming through her mind over the past day.

"Tavra! Will you let me get in the house before you start telling me so many stories? You need to learn how to be by yourself. Go to your room!" her mom said.

Tavra replayed those scenes over and over in her mind. Hours of crying lasted through the night and nights turned to days. Her crying just wouldn't stop. "Nobody loves me! Noooobody loves me!" she cried.

"Honey, please stop saying that. We love you. I don't want to hear you say that ever again," her mom said one day.

Tavra respected her mom's wishes. Rather than saying, "Nobody loves me," Tavra continued her daily crying, but began saying, "Nobody likes me," instead.

And, by now, everyone was sick of hearing her cry and everyone ignored her.
One day, a new girl came into the neighborhood with so many beautiful bracelets on her arms.

When she saw Tavra crying, she said, "What's wrong, littl girl?"
Jada, a neighborhood girl who was clearly tired of all the crying, said, "She thinks nobody likes her."

9

The new girl said, "Well, I like you, little girl. Here, have a bracelet." With that, Tavra quieted herself and wiped her eyes for the first time in a long time. She heard Jada exclaim, "Shoot, don't nobody like me, either! Can I have a free bracelet, too?"

Later that night, when Tavra closed her eyes for bed, a beautiful princess appeared. The princess looked just like Tavra, but was a little older and glowed with radiant light.

"Hello, Tavra!"
"Hello, there. Who are you?"
"I am Princess Vati. I have been trying to reach you, but you couldn't hear me because you have been crying so much."

12

"You've been trying to reach me?" Tavra asked.
"Yes," said Princess Vati.
"Why?" Tavra asked.

"Because I wanted to tell you that you are loved beyond measure. Look at your third toe on your left foot. How do you think that got there?" Princess Vati asked.

"Huh? I don't know," Tavra said.

"Look at that teeny, tiny mole on the bottom of your left hand. How do you think that got there?" Princess Vati asked.

"I don't know," Tavra said.

15

"Because God put it there. Our all-powerful, all-loving God who creates all things thought it would be simply delightful to create YOU. You have been made perfectly in every way—from your special smile, to your third toe, to the way that you dance when you think no one is looking.

You are deeply loved and there is nothing that you can ever do to change that." Princess Vati glowed even more as she spoke.

"So, God loves me always?"
Tavra asked.
"Always," said Princess Vati.
"Does God love everyone?" Tavra
asked.

"Each and every one of us," Princess Vati replied as she waved her wand, and like magic, they started flying towards the moon.

"Well, I might believe that God loves me," Tavra said, excited to be sitting on the moon. "But no one else does," she said as she began to mope again.

"But don't you see? That's not true. What did your mother tell you?" asked Princess Vati.

"She told me they love me and that she doesn't want to hear me say that no one loves me anymore. But, if she loves me, why doesn't she want to know how I really feel? Why does she want me to keep my feelings to myself?" Tavra really wanted to know.

"She wants you to stop saying it because she knows that the more you say it, the more you are going to believe it," Princess Vati replied.
"But, even when I am not saying it, I am still thinking it. And I am still believing it," Tavra explained.

"Yes, this is true. And this is where you have to come in and save yourself," Princess Vati said.

"Save myself?" Tavra asked.

"Yes. Save yourself. It was never that the other people around you don't love you. It is that you are not feeling love towards yourself.

When you are not feeling love towards yourself, it makes it very hard for you to feel the love that is coming from other people," Princess Vati explained.

"So, I have to love myself?" Tavra asked.
"Yes, you must love yourself, Tavra," Princess Vati confirmed.
"But how do I do that?" Tavra asked.

24

"It's very simple, Tavra. You already know that you were created perfectly and purposely. Now, all you have to do is decide," Princess Vati answered.

"Decide?" Tavra said.

"Yes, decide. When you decide, you cut off all other choices. So, you have to decide that you love yourself," said Princess Vati.

"If you loved yourself, what would you say to yourself?" Princess Vati asked.
"Well, I would tell me that I love me," Tavra said in a soft voice.

26

"Good. Can you tell yourself that now?"
Princess Vati handed Tavra a mirror.
Tavra looked into the mirror and said, "I
love you."

"What else would you say to yourself?"
asked Princess Vati.
"That God made me perfectly just the
way I am?" Tavra said, sounding a little
unsure of herself.

27

"Yes, tell yourself that now," Princess Vati said.
"God made you perfectly just the way you are," Tavra said.

28

"What else would you say?" Princess Vati asked. "I am beautiful and funny and I love to play with bunnies. I am smart and classy and still a bit sassy. But even if none of this were true, Tavra, I love you just for being you!"

Elated, Princess Vati said, "Bravo! Bravo, Tavra! See, you just decide. And make this same decision every day–to love yourself, Tavra, for just being you!"

"Yes, I understand now. Love myself, for just being me. I love you, Tavra! I love me! I will remember to decide again every day that I love me," Tavra beamed with joy.

"You got it!" Princess Vati said as she started to fade away.
"Wait, where are you going?" Tavra asked as she realized she was back in her room.

"Never far away, Tavra," Princess Vati assured her.
"But will I ever see you again?" Tavra asked.
"I am always here for you. I am always whispering
in your ear. But remember, you can only hear me
when you are quiet..."

The next morning, Tavra awakened with a smile on her face. She had not felt like this in a long time. She jumped out of bed with a song in her heart. Her family's ears perked up as they heard Tavra singing a joyful song.

"Do you hear that?" Niles exclaimed. Everyone ran to give Tavra a big hug. They were happy to have her back!

Tavra thought about her visitor the night before.
"She was right. All I have to do is love myself.
Then I will feel the love from everyone else around
me, too." Tavra winked at herself as she gazed in
her own eyes in the mirror.

34

Journal with Tavra

On these pages you can use your imagination and draw, color, and write!

me and Princess cats ♡

BY TAVRA

At the beginning of the story,
Tavra thinks no one loves her.
Draw a face or write how you think
she was feeling.

How you ever felt left out? How
did it feel?

_____

_____

The new girl asked Tavra what was wrong and gave her a bracelet. What type of action was this? (Circle all that apply)

Kind   Caring   Selfish   Giving   Mean

Draw and color a bracelet.

What is something kind that you have done for someone? How did it make them feel? How did you feel?

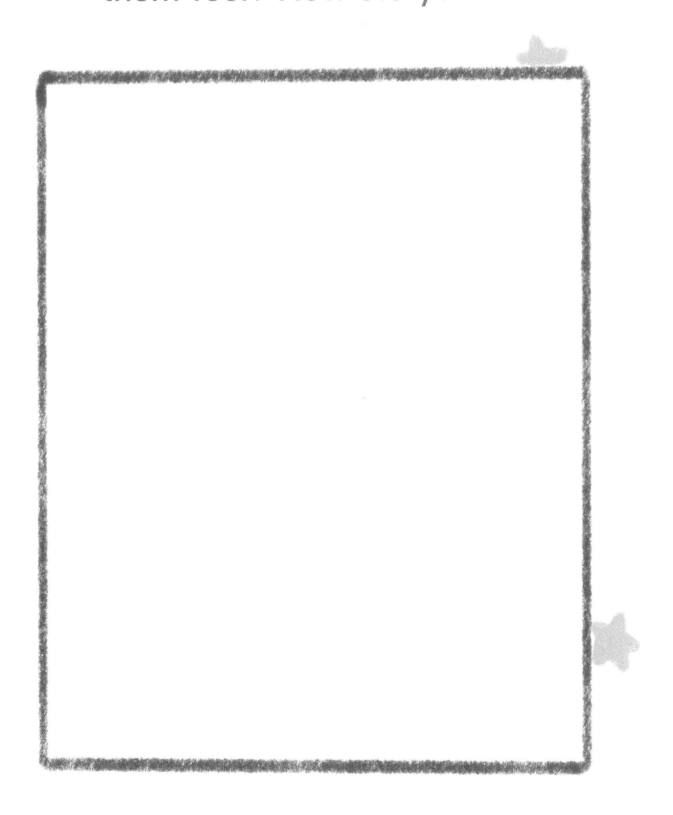

Princess Vati told Tavra that she had to love herself everyday.

When you look in the mirror what loving words can you say to yourself?

Write the reasons why YOU love YOU.
Color in the mirror.

I LOVE ME!

For the Adult Reader
Guided Discussion Points

From Pages 1-2
- How was Tavra FEELING at the start of the story?
    - (Tell them some feeling words, if needed: Happy, sad, excited, mad, etc.) *She was feeling sad.*
- How do you know how she was feeling?
    - *Because she was crying.*
- Show me a SAD face.
    - They can either draw it or make their faces look sad.
- Did some of the other children try to help Tavra feel better?
    - *Yes*
- What did they do?
    - *They told her they love her.* [But she was too upset to really hear them.]
- Have you ever helped someone to feel better? What did you do?

From Pages 3-4
- Why did Tavra think no one loved her?
    - *Her brothers said mean things to her and laughed ("Get away from us, you buck-toothed beaver!")*
    - *The older girls didn't want her around because she didn't know any dances or cheers.*
    - *Tavra always missed the ball when it was her turn to bat, so no one wanted her on their team.*
- Did you know that even when you are just trying to be funny, that saying mean things to a person can hurt their feelings?
- What are some *kind* things that you can say to a person?

From Pages 9-10
- Why do you think Tavra finally stopped crying when the girl selling bracelets stopped by?
    - *Someone took the time to really see Tavra and ask her what was wrong. She showed Tavra she cared. She was kind, and, even though she didn't know Tavra, she went above and beyond and offered Tavra a gift.*

From Pages 11-12
- Why do you think Princess Vati looked just like Tavra except she was older and had a glow?
    - *Princess Vati IS Tavra. She is a part of Tavra that Tavra does not know yet. We all are more than what we see when we look in the mirror. When you look in the mirror, there are many things that you cannot see. You cannot see your thoughts. You cannot see how strong you are. You cannot see how loving or kind you are. You cannot see how funny you are. You cannot see how smart you are. As you get older, you will start to become aware of more and more parts of yourself that have always been there—like your confidence, your strength, your courage, your ability to love everyone, your wisdom, your power, and your light or inner glow.*

From Pages 15-16

- Why was Princess Vati trying to reach Tavra?
  - *To tell her that she is loved beyond measure. God made her perfectly. God loves her more than she could ever imagine and there is nothing that could ever change that. And, God loves each and everyone of us.*

From Pages 23-24
- Why does Princess Vati tell Tavra to save herself?
  - *Tavra is looking at how everyone outside of her is behaving, and based on their behaviors, she feels that no one likes her and that makes her very sad. But Princess Vati wants her to know that it is much more important how Tavra feels about herself than how everyone else feels about her. If Tavra does not feel love for herself, it will make it hard for her to feel love from the people around her.*

From Pages 25-26
- What did Princess Vati tell Tavra she needed to do to save herself?
  - *Decide. Decide that she loves herself.*
- What does it mean to decide or to make a decision?
  - *To cut off all other choices.*

From Pages 27-28
- Look into the mirror (or pretend to look into the mirror). Gaze into your own eyes. Smile at yourself. Tell yourself that you love yourself. Tell yourself that you were made perfectly, just the way you are.
- What else can you say to yourself? Tell yourself some of the things that you love about yourself: Are you kind? Funny? Smart? Beautiful? Can you draw? Play football? Play video games? Do you like animals? Babies? Are you helpful? Can you run fast? Do you like to ride your bike? Can you write your letters? Are you good at math or reading? Can you color? Can you cook?
- And, tell yourself: "Even if none of those things were true, I love you for just being you."
- Give the children a big round of applause and have them applaud themselves.
- Remind them that Princess Vati said, "You just decide. And make this same decision every day—to love yourself for just being you."

Author's Bio:

Arvat McClaine is a world-traveler and has spoken internationally about how to move from a life of struggle to one where your biggest dreams come true. Arvat co-founded the first independent African-centered school in the state of Virginia (pre-K-8th grade), and has worked extensively with both children and adults in the fields of mental health and personal development.

Arvat literally married "the boy next door." She and her husband, Harry Watkins, have been best friends for about 40 years. They are both avid entrepreneurs and adventurers, having traveled to all 7 continents, jumped out of an airplane, and climbed Mt. Kilimanjaro together. Additionally, Arvat has walked barefoot across a hot bed of coals and is an endurance athlete. Her greatest passion is igniting the "magic" that we all have within to live our best lives.

CPSIA information can be obtained
at www.ICGtesting.com
Printed in the USA
BVHW021324300321
603711BV00015B/1543